DATE DUE

THIS BOOK BELONGS TO

Ernestine J.

Moore - Drolet

AUG 2 2 2000

THE
CHRISTMAS
BEAR

Paul and Henrietta Stickland

Lester Publishing Limited

Little Bear lived at the top of the world.

One Christmas night he left his parents in their snuggly den to explore. Little Bear followed his nose. It led him over the hill to a hole in the snow. I wonder who lives down there? thought Little Bear.

He followed his nose further and further into the hole until . . .

Little Bear fell in!

Down . . . down . . .

down he fell.

He landed . . . *bump*! at the bottom.

'Little Bear!' said a friendly voice. 'What a tumble!'

Little Bear peeped between his paws and saw a jolly man smiling down at him.

'I'm Father Christmas,' said Father Christmas. 'How kind of you to drop in. I could do with some help.'

'Letters, letters, letters!' said Father Christmas as he showed Little Bear the sorting room. 'So many children, so many presents!'

Little Bear helped sort some letters. But there was so much else to look at – and where was that penguin going? he wondered.

'The workshop!' said Father Christmas proudly as he hurried Little Bear into the next room. 'We make all the toys here – teddies, trains, dinosaurs . . . you name it. I've designed one or two myself,' admitted Father Christmas with a chuckle.

Little Bear wanted to make some toys, too.

Then Father Christmas took Little Bear into a room full of noisy machinery.

'This is the North Pole,' he shouted. 'We use it to make our own electricity. It's quite simple.'

Little Bear nodded his head as if he understood, but he was really watching the penguin.

'**H**ere's a lovely job for you,' said Father Christmas, as they arrived in yet another room. 'Testing all the toys!'

Little Bear was so excited, he couldn't think where to start.

'**T**esting, testing!' said Little Bear as he squeezed a teddy's tummy.

'*Grrr!*' growled the teddy.

'You'll do,' said Little Bear. 'Now where's that penguin?'

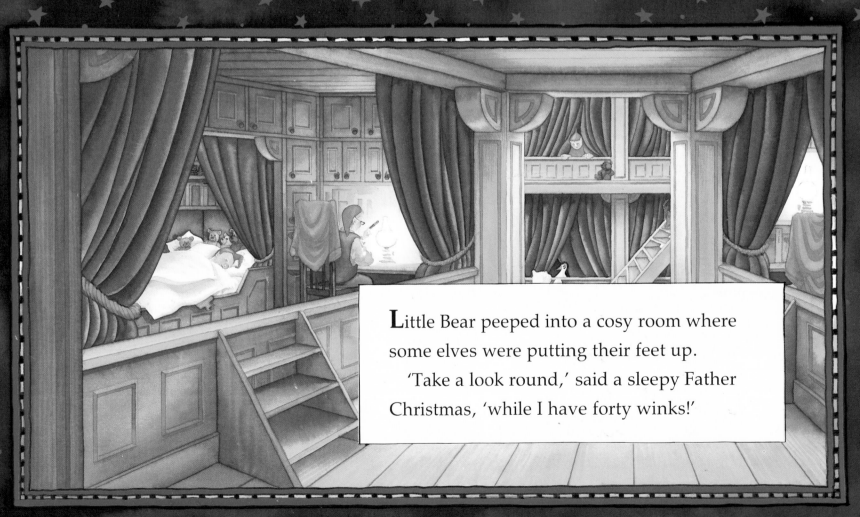

Little Bear peeped into a cosy room where some elves were putting their feet up.

'Take a look round,' said a sleepy Father Christmas, 'while I have forty winks!'

Little Bear followed his nose to the kitchen.
There was a delicious smell of baking. Soon
it was time for tea. Little Bear sniffed.
 'Fish and ice cream,' he said. '*Grrreat!*'

'**B**ack to work again,' said Father Christmas, taking Little Bear into the storeroom. There were lists to be checked and toys to be found for children all over the world. It kept Little Bear busy for hours.

I wonder if there's a present for me? he thought.

'Present wrapping department,' Father Christmas informed Little Bear when they got there.

Little Bear had never seen so many presents and so much wrapping paper.

'Not long now,' said Father Christmas. 'Look. There goes a sack of toys down to my sleigh.'

Father Christmas and Little Bear went to the stable.

'Nearly time to go,' said Father Christmas to his reindeer. 'And more cats to feed, I see.'

'Mice, too,' said Little Bear.

'Well, Happy Christmas, cats and mice,' said Father Christmas. 'Now, we must be off!'

Father Christmas reached into a pile of presents and gave one to Little Bear. 'This one is for you,' he said. 'My Little *Christmas* Bear.'

'Oh, thank you!' cried Little Bear.

'I . . . er, made it myself,' said Father Christmas. 'I think it's rather special. Now, climb in, Little Bear.'

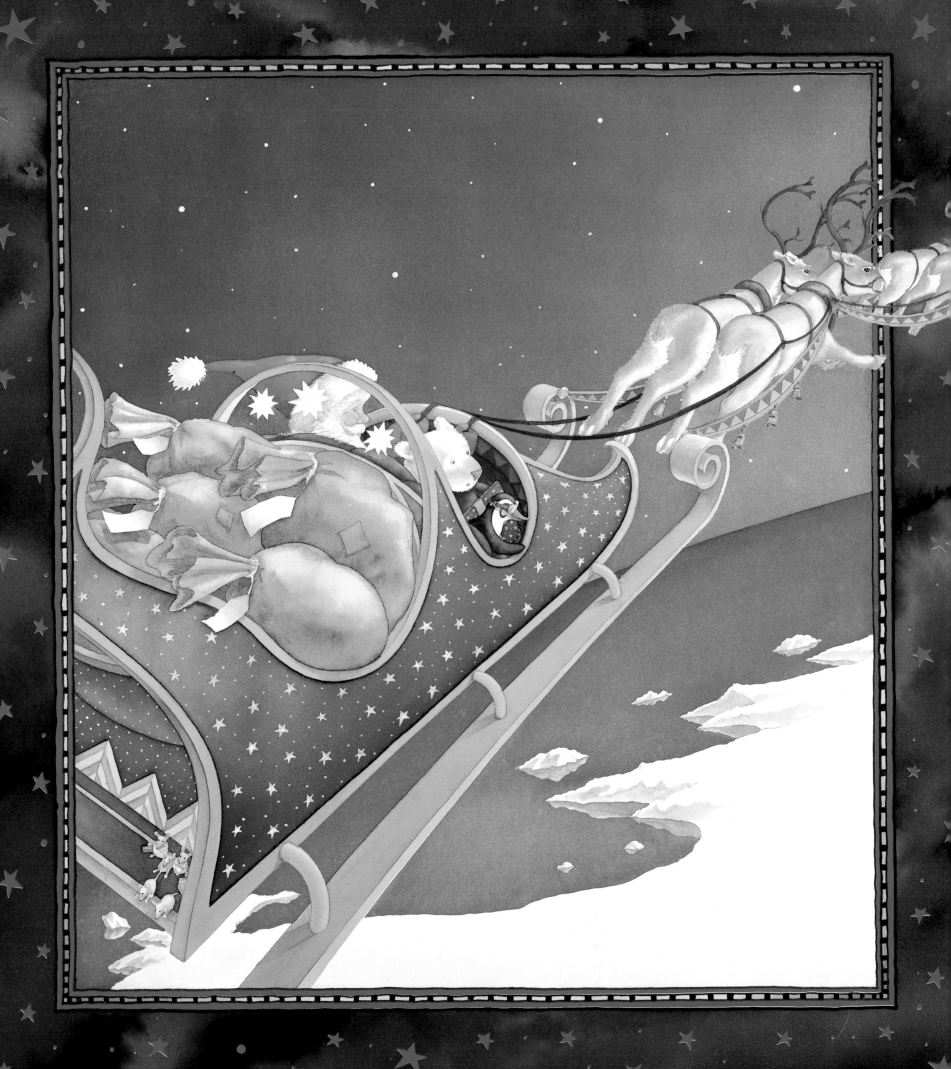

'First stop, the top of the world!' said Father Christmas.
And in a wink they were safely home.
    'Open your present, Little Bear,' said Father Christmas.
    'It's a book, and it's all about ME!' said Little Bear.
    'Time I was on my way,' said Father Christmas.

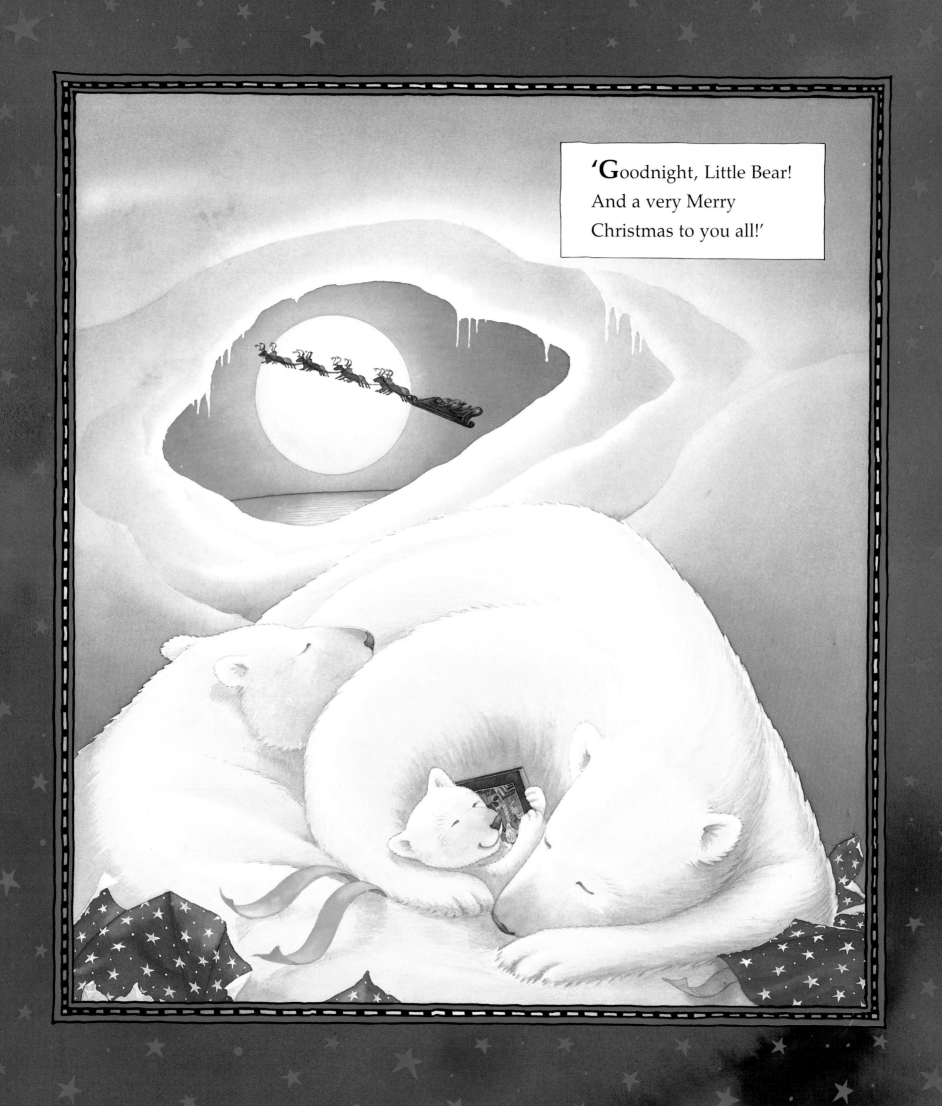

'Goodnight, Little Bear!
And a very Merry
Christmas to you all!'

For my grampa, artist and illustrator
Geoffrey Squire
P.S.

For Emily, Little Etta, Katie, Danda,
Erica, and Thomas, with much love
H.S.

First published in Canada in 1993 by Lester Publishing Limited,
56 The Esplanade, Toronto, Canada M5E 1A7
Originally published in the United States in 1993 by Dutton Children's Books,
a division of Penguin Books USA Inc., New York

Canadian Cataloguing in Publication Data

Stickland, Henrietta
The Christmas bear

1st Canadian ed.
ISBN 1-895555-46-9

I. Stickland, Paul. II. Title.
PZ7.S854Ch   1993   j813'.54   C93-094301-5

Printed and bound in Italy

93 94 95 96 1 2 3 4 5